To Betty,
"An elect lady" with a
missionary's heart.
With love,
George Ann Broch
Dec. 1998

A child asks…

What Does Dying Mean?

by
Lake Pylant Monhollon

illustrated by
George Ann Brock

REFLECTION
PUBLISHING

Copyright © 1998 by Lake Pylant Monhollon
Illustrations © 1998 by George Ann Brock
Typography by Debra H. Warr
Printed in the U.S.A. All rights reserved.
Published by Reflection Publishing
1 Hendrick Drive, Abilene, Texas 79602
www.reflectionpublishing.com

Library of Congress Cataloging-in-Publication Data
Monhollon, Lake Pylant
  What Does Dying Mean? /Lake Pylant Monhollon.
—1st ed.

Summary: A fully illustrated book to help young
children cope with death.
ISBN 0-9657561-1-4   LC 97-91836

This little book is dedicated to
my own mom and dad, who are already in heaven –
Agnes Durant Pylant and
Lake Ruble Pylant

and

Jeanne Henry, who urged me to write it.

Look down.

Do you see a leg?

Your leg?

That's part of your earthsuit.

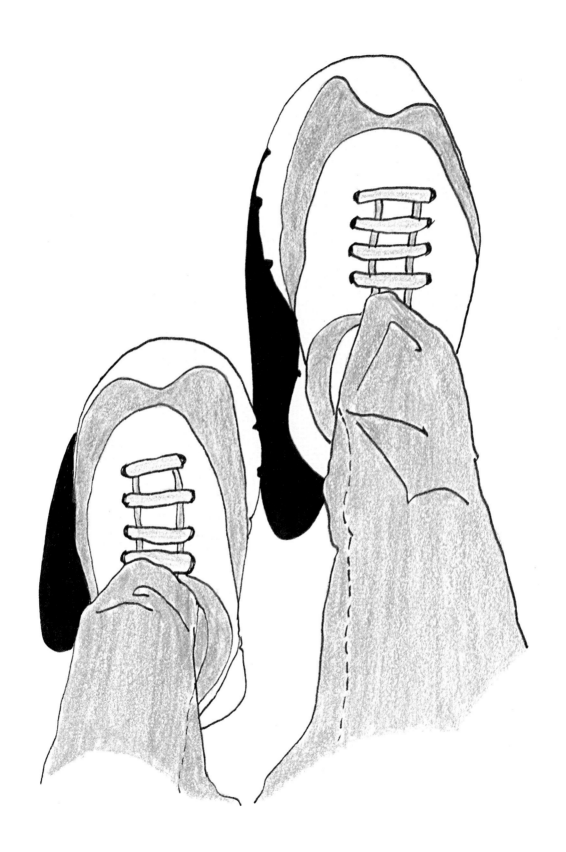

Look in the mirror.

That's more of your earthsuit.

Astronauts need spacesuits to live in space.
We need earthsuits to live on Earth.
Scientists invented spacesuits.

God invented earthsuits.

Here you are in your earthsuit.
God created your earthsuit
        with eyes to see
                and ears to hear,
                    a nose to smell,
                        a mouth for eating,
                            fingers for touching,
                                feet and legs for walking.

That way, the *real* you can enjoy
        the beautiful world that God made.

When you first got your earthsuit, it was very,
very small —

— and not all that useful.

But it grew.

It will keep growing until it is as big as your parents' earthsuits.

Spacesuits do not grow.

When a spacesuit gets torn or broken, it cannot fix itself.

Your earthsuit is much, much better. It can fix itself.

Most of the time.

Sometimes an earthsuit gets too broken to fix itself. And even the best earthsuits grow old and wear out.

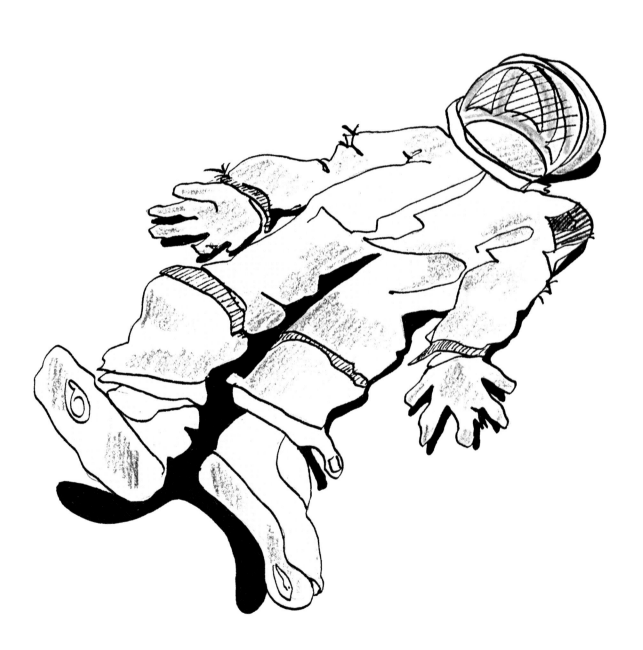

An earthsuit is not meant to last forever. An astronaut only needs a spacesuit when he is in space.

You only need your earthsuit while you are on earth.

(Earth is the world we live in.)

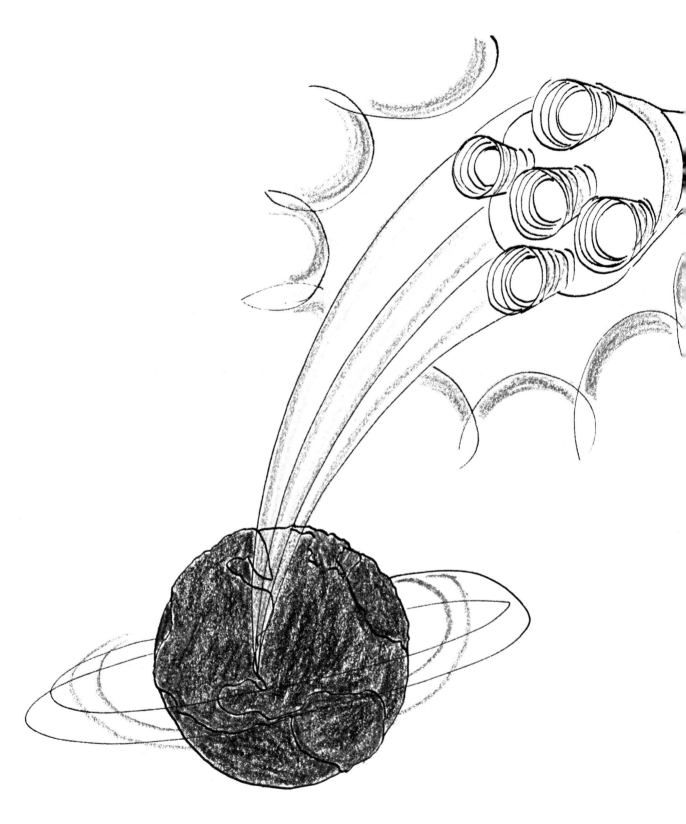

God made the world for you and your earthsuit.

God gave you parents to take care of you.

God gave you food to eat and water to drink.

God made birds and animals and friends.

He made the world beautiful. He made trees and flowers and beaches.

He made other people for you to love.

He made people for you to help.

Oh, there is so much to see and do!

When you are little, it seems like your life on Earth will be very, very long.

The days go by.

The weeks, months, and years go by.

You go to school and learn about the Earth. You learn about your earthsuit.

You need to learn about the Earth and about your earthsuit.

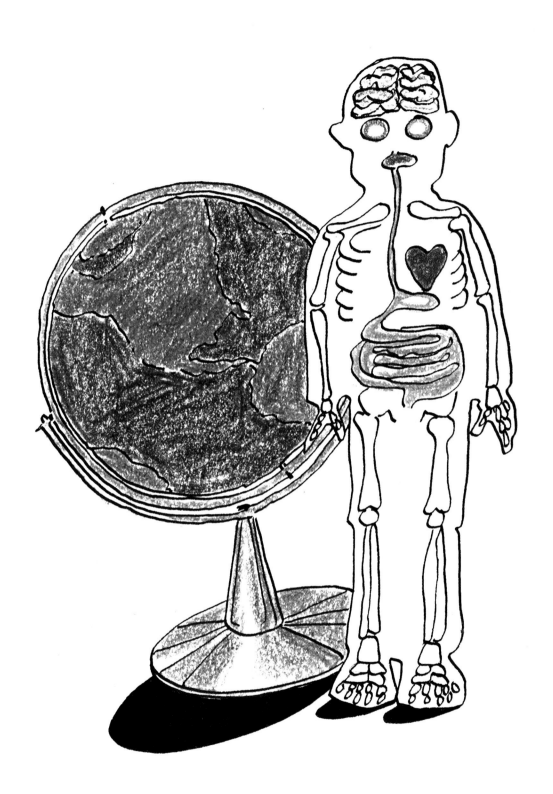

There is something else you need to learn.

You need to learn about the real you that lives inside your earthsuit.

You need to learn about God and how much He loves you.

And you need to learn about Jesus.

Jesus lived with God. Then Jesus put on an earthsuit to come visit us. He came to invite us to come and live with him when our earthsuits wear out.

Someday it will be time to take off your earthsuit. An astronaut does not need his spacesuit when he goes home. He takes it off.

You will not need an earthsuit when you go home. Someday you will leave your earthsuit and go to your Real Life with God. There you will not need an earthsuit, because you will be in your Real Home.
Your forever–and–ever home. It is the home you were really made for. When you are at home in Heaven, you will not need your earthsuit anymore.

Everyone does not go to Heaven at the same time.

Some people will leave their earthsuits before you do. When people you love die, it means their earthsuits have worn out or quit working. You will miss them very much, because you loved to be with them. But it is just the earthsuits that died. The persons you love are still very much alive. Your loved one has gone to the Real world – Heaven – and will be **very** happy. The one you love who has already gone to Heaven knows you will be coming, too, someday.

When you leave your earthsuit, some of your friends will still be in their earthsuits. Some of your family will still be in their earthsuits. They will bury your empty earthsuit, because you do not need it anymore.

They will be sad, because they miss you. But they know that they will be coming to be with you soon.

Heaven is more exciting and wonderful than anything you ever dreamed. Everything is beautiful.

Nothing ever wears out. People never get hurt or sick or grow old or die. If your earthsuit on Earth was not perfect, you will be free of it now. You will be more free and happy than you have ever been.

There is so much to do there that no one ever gets bored. Yet there is plenty of time for each other. No one is lonesome or cries. It is never too hot or too cold. No one is ever tired or hungry.

No one ever has to be frightened again. There are no storms and no mean people. Heaven is a totally safe place.

Many wonderful people are there and they will know you and love you. They are expecting you and they look forward to seeing you.

You will be able to walk and talk with Jesus. You will be able to visit with Noah and Abraham and George Washington. All your questions will be answered. Your grandmother and grandfather will be there. Their parents and grandparents will be there, too, if they loved God and trusted His son, Jesus. In fact, everyone who has ever lived and trusted Jesus will be there.

Most exciting of all is that God is there, and you will meet Him. He is the powerful One who made you. He loves you more than anyone in the whole world.

And guess what! It's a life that will never end. You will never have to leave it. You will never be separated from your family or friends again.

It will be your home forever!